This Notebook Belongs To

....

Made in the USA
Middletown, DE
24 October 2023

41335577R00068